MW01179031

adapted by Farrah McDoogle
based on the screenplay written by Chris Nee
illustrated by Jared Osterhold

Based on the TV series *OLIVIA*™ as seen on Nickelodeon™

SIMON SPOTLIGHT
An imprint of Simon & Schuster Children's Publishing Division
New York London Toronto Sydney
1230 Avenue of the Americas, New York, New York 10020

For information about special discounts for bulk purchases,
please contact Simon & Schuster Special Sales at 1-866-506-1949 or business@simonandschuster.com.
Manufactured in the United States of America 0911 CWM
4 6 8 10 9 7 5 ISBN 978-1-4424-3061-7

"Ooo-loo-loo-loo!" called Mrs. Hoggenmuller as she stood in front of the blackboard. All the students looked around, puzzled. And then she did it again. "Ooo-loo—loo-loo!"

"Are you okay, Mrs. Hoggenmuller?" asked Olivia.

"Yes, of course. Today is Turkey Day, and I am celebrating by talking turkey!" said their teacher.

"When I was young, I always wanted a turkey as a pet, but my parents were goldfish people," she recalled.

"I want to learn to talk turkey too," said Olivia.

"That's great, Olivia!" Mrs. Hoggenmuller exclaimed. "You'll just need to practice. I should know—I am a champion turkey talker, and it does require some practice!"

Later that day Olivia practiced talking turkey. "Ooo-loo-la-la-loo!" she called. She waited, but no turkeys appeared. She tried her turkey call again: "Ooo-loo-la-la-loo!"

"Still no turkeys," Ian told her. "But Perry came when you called."

"I think I need to find my really special turkey call," Olivia told Ian. "I just need more practice."

And so Olivia kept practicing. After a lot of practice something happened. Olivia planted her feet firmly on the ground, threw back her head, and called out "Oo-loo-la-la-loo!" This time her turkey call was just right. Olivia heard a noise in the bushes . . .

And out popped a *turkey*!

"I did it!" Olivia shouted to Ian. "I can talk to turkeys!"

"Dad, guess what?" Olivia asked as she came into the kitchen. "I can talk to turkeys!"

"That's nice," said Father as he tried to feed Baby William. "I can do a pretty good 'gobble-gobble' myself!"

"Let me show you how it's done!" Olivia said. "This is how you talk to turkeys: Oo-loo-la-la-loo!"

Olivia had barely finished her call when the turkey appeared at her side.

"Olivia, that's a turkey!" cried Father.

"I know," said Olivia. "I have a way with animals!"

The turkey ran through the house and into Mother's office. "There's a turkey in here!" called Mother, shouting over the sounds of things being knocked over in her office.

"Let me handle this," answered Olivia. "Oo-loo-la-la-loo!" she called. Her obedient turkey appeared at her side . . . but not before making even more of a mess.
"He says he's sorry?" Olivia told her parents.

Mother and Father explained to Olivia that she couldn't keep the turkey as a pet. Even though Olivia loved her new turkey friend, she understood. So they put the turkey outside. A few moments later the doorbell rang. Olivia ran to answer the door and in walked the turkey.

"You really do have a way with animals," Ian told Olivia. "That turkey really likes you!"

"I know what I have to do," Olivia replied. "I have to find someone the turkey will like even more. Someone who wants a turkey for a pet . . ." Olivia thought about it. And then the perfect solution came to her.

The next day Olivia brought her new friend to school with her.

"My goodness, what a handsome turkey!" Mrs. Hoggenmuller exclaimed when she saw him. Then she cleared her throat and called "Oo-loo-la-la-loo!" It was the perfect turkey call, and for the first time the turkey tore his eyes away from Olivia and focused on Mrs. Hoggenmuller.

"It's a perfect match," Olivia whispered to Julian. "He really, really likes her!" Mrs. Hoggenmuller asked Olivia if she could adopt the turkey, and Olivia was happy to agree.

"Are you sure you don't mind?" Mrs. Hoggenmuller asked.

"I'm sure," Olivia assured her. "Oh, and I think he likes popcorn!" she added.

"He can have all the popcorn he wants!" replied Mrs. Hoggenmuller.

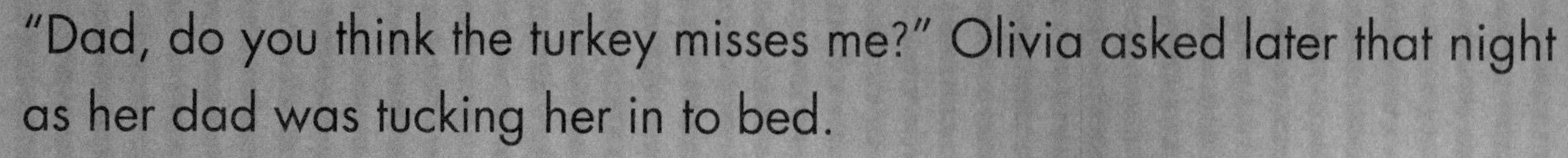

"Dad, do you think the turkey misses me?" Olivia asked later that night as her dad was tucking her in to bed.

"I'm sure he does," Father replied. "Now go to sleep, Olivia. *Gobble-gobble!*"

"Oo-loo-la-la-loo!" said Olivia.